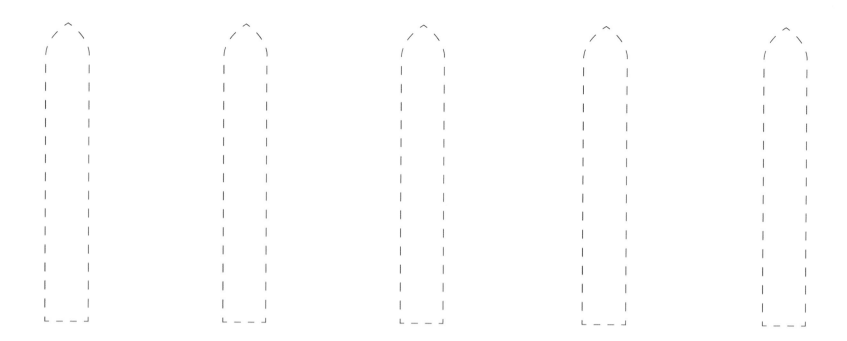

To Candela, Mateo, and Silvia . . . gracias.

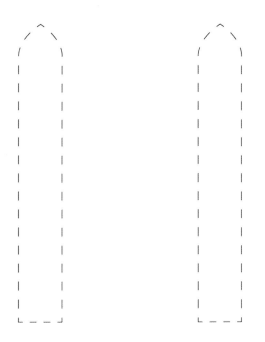

THE KING OF NOTHING

GURIDI

TRANSLATED FROM THE SPANISH BY SAUL ENDOR

The New York Review Children's Collection
New York

IT'S NO SMALL THING TO BE THE KING OF NOTHING.
IT MAY BE THE MOST IMPORTANT THING IN THE WORLD,
SAID MIMO THE FIRST (AS HE CHOSE TO BE KNOWN).

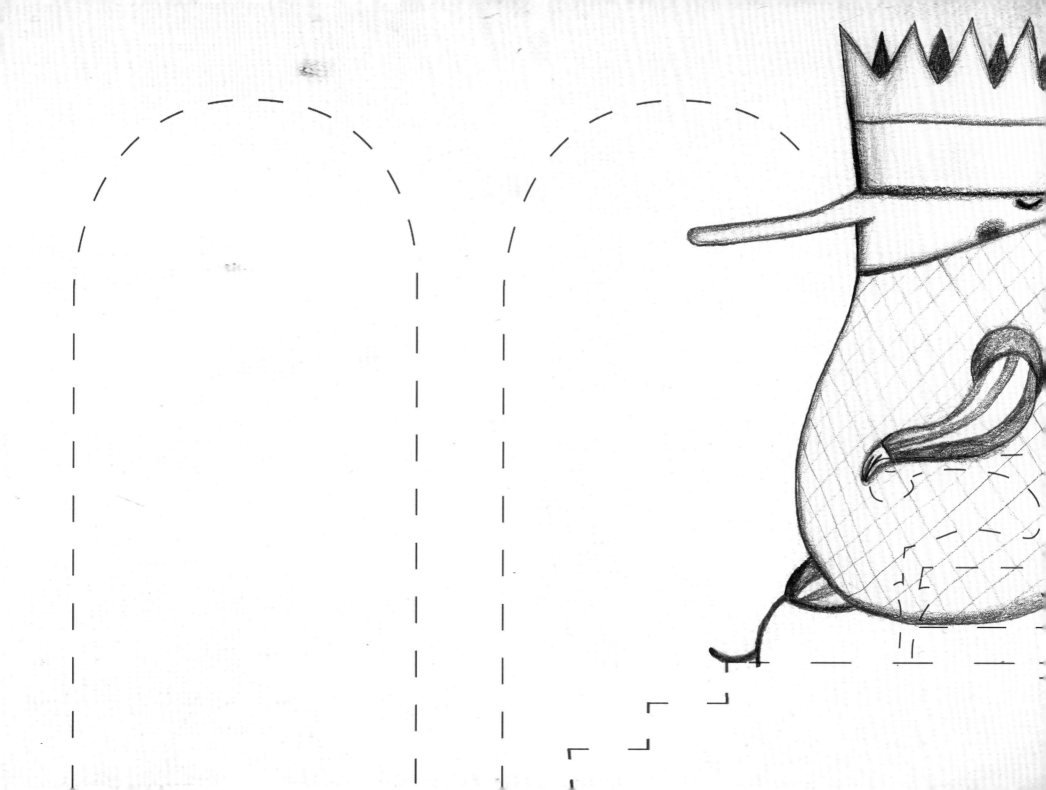

EVERY DAY MIMO THE FIRST, THE GREAT MIMO THE FIRST, SET OUT FROM HIS ENORMOUS CASTLE TO TRAVEL AROUND HIS KINGDOM ON ONE OF THE MORE THAN ONE HUNDRED AND FIFTY HORSES HE CALLED HIS OWN.

AND TWICE A WEEK AT THE HEAD OF HIS IMMENSE ARMY HE PARADED
FROM ONE END OF HIS KINGDOM TO THE OTHER
SO THAT HIS PEOPLE COULD SEE HOW VERY GREAT HE WAS.

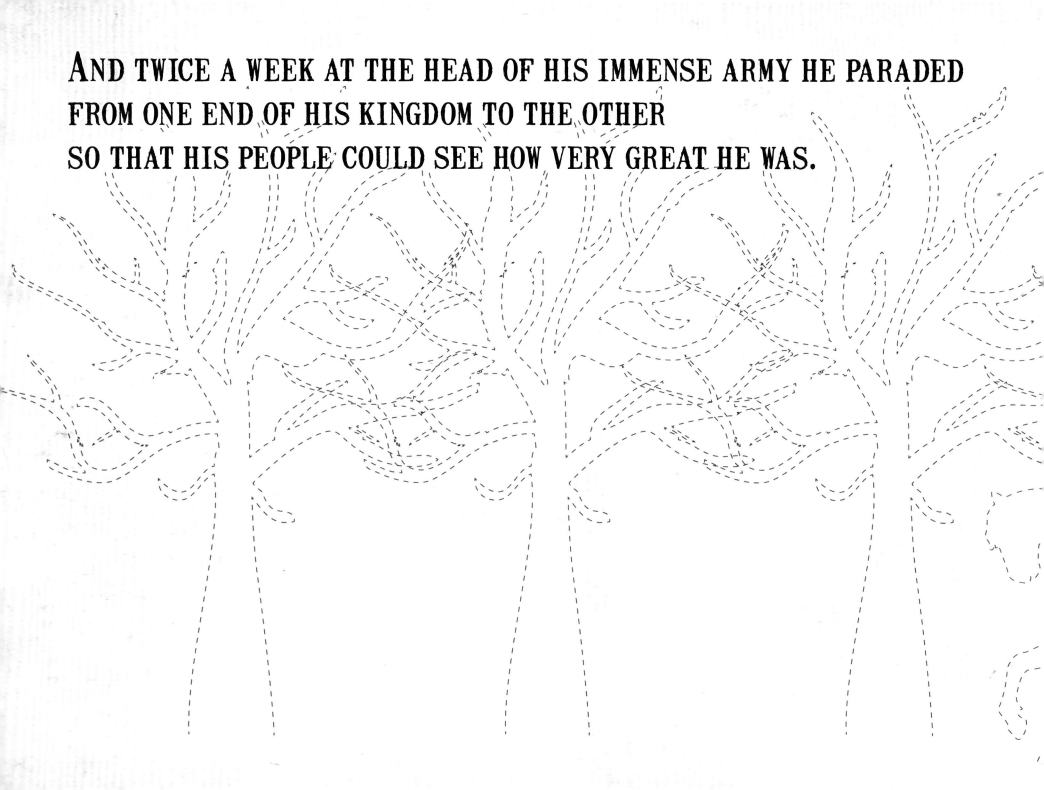

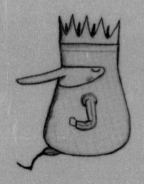

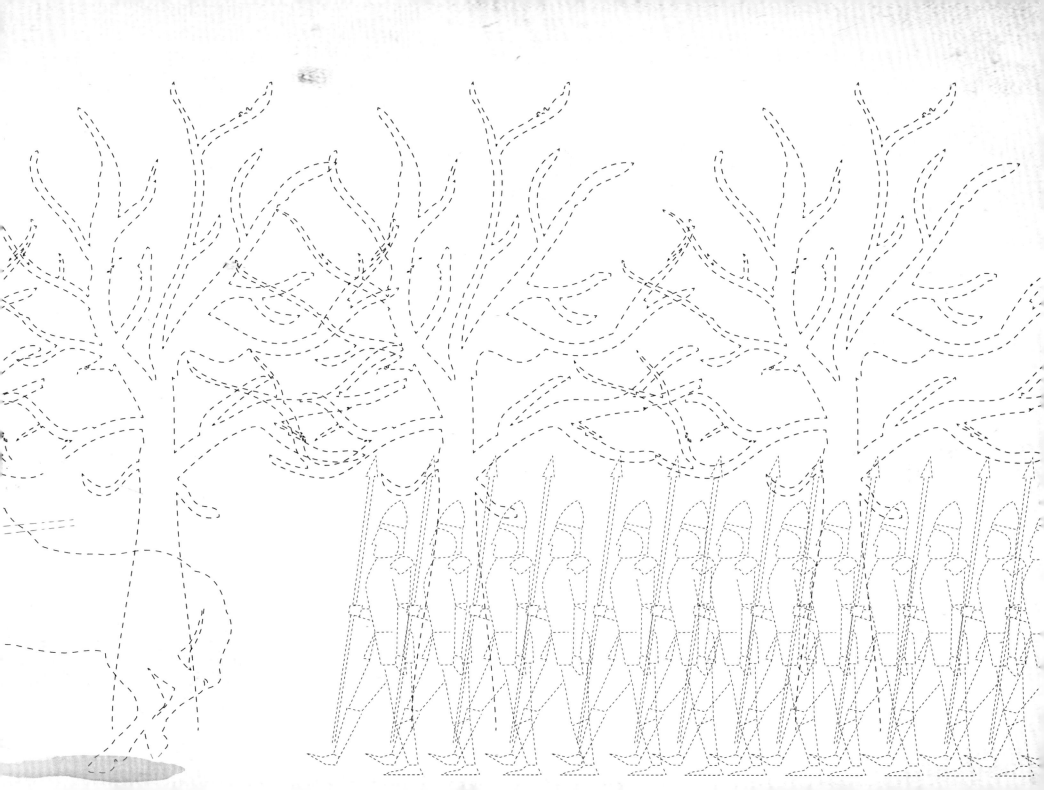

COME SUNSET HE CLIMBED TO THE TOP OF THE TALLEST TOWER
AND FROM THERE HE SURVEYED THE WHOLE OF THE MARVELOUS COUNTRY
OVER WHICH HE, AND ONLY HE, HELD ABSOLUTE DOMINION.

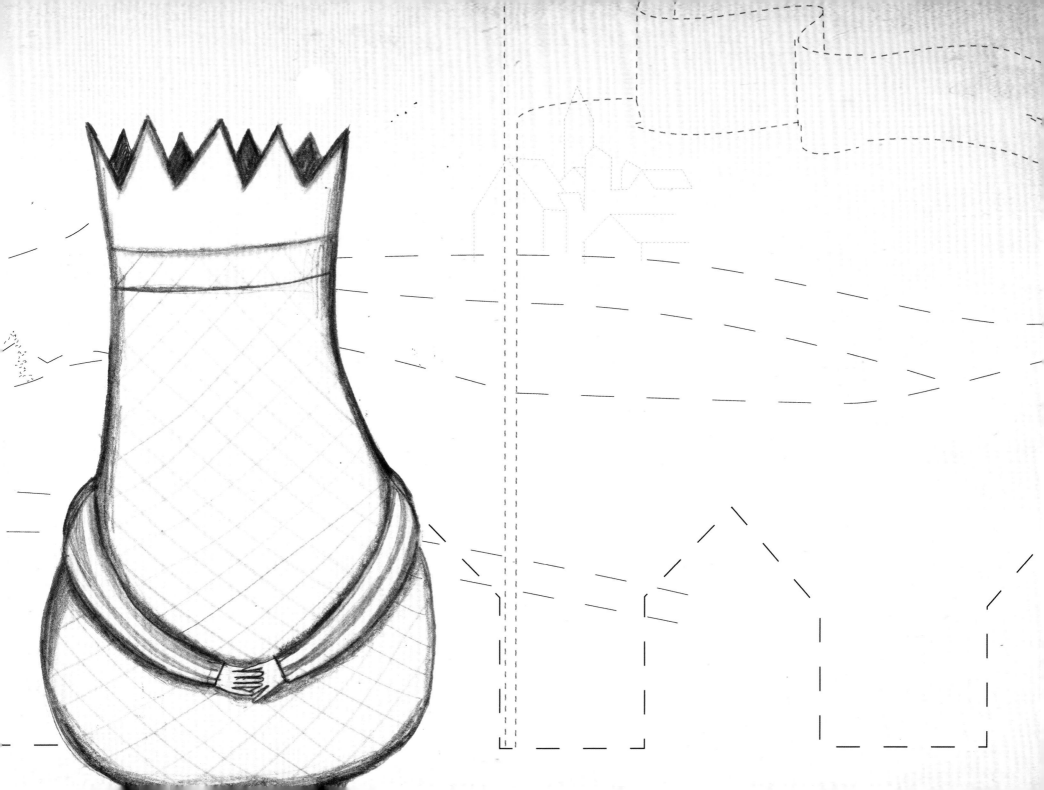

ONE DAY, HOWEVER, ON ONE OF HIS WEEKLY REVIEWS,
MIMO THE FIRST ENCOUNTERED THE ONE THING THAT MORE
THAN ANYTHING HAD NO PLACE AT ALL IN ALL HIS REALM.
THERE, BEFORE HIS EYES, WAS *SOMETHING*.

SOME-THING? SOME-THING? HERE-IN-MY-VERY-
OWN-KING-DOM-OF-NOTH-ING, SOME-THING?
(THIS IS HOW THE KING ALWAYS TALKED, STRESSING HIS EVERY
SYLLABLE. TO MAKE A MARK ON HISTORY, HE KNEW, KINGS
HAD TO TALK LIKE THAT.)

THIS-CAN-NOT-BE! THIS-CAN-NOT-BE! HE SAID AND SAID AGAIN.
HE WAS BRIMMING OVER WITH INDIGNATION
(INDIGNATION, HE KNEW, WAS JUST THE THING FOR A KING).

SOME-WITCH-HAS-DONE-THIS-THING!
OR-THE-DE-VIL!
SOME-CUR-SED-WITCH!

HE GOT DOWN OFF HIS HORSE AND ORDERED ALL THOSE FANTASTIC
SOLDIERS OF HIS TO SEIZE THE *SOMETHING* AND HAUL IT OFF TO
PRISON RIGHT NOW.
(NONE OF THEM DARED TO. MIMO THE FIRST HAD TO CAPTURE THE
SOMETHING ALL BY HIMSELF. MUMBLING AND GRUMBLING, HE LOCKED
IT BEHIND BARS.)

MIMO THE FIRST WAS REALLY WORRIED.

WHAT IF *SOMETHINGS* STARTED TURNING UP ALL OVER THE PLACE?

WHAT IF THEY SEIZE MY CASTLE? WHAT IF . . . ?

AND WITH ONE *WHAT IF* AFTER ANOTHER,

THE KING FELL ASLEEP.

IN HIS DREAMS, TERRIFYING SOMETHINGS WERE TRANSFORMED

INTO MARVELOUS NOTHINGS AT THE STROKE OF A SWORD.

WHEN HE WOKE UP HE DISCOVERED THAT THE *SOMETHING* HAD VANISHED.

WHAT? HOW? WHEN? WHERE? HE YELLED.

HE SEARCHED AND SEARCHED, BUT IT WAS NO USE, HE FOUND NOTHING.

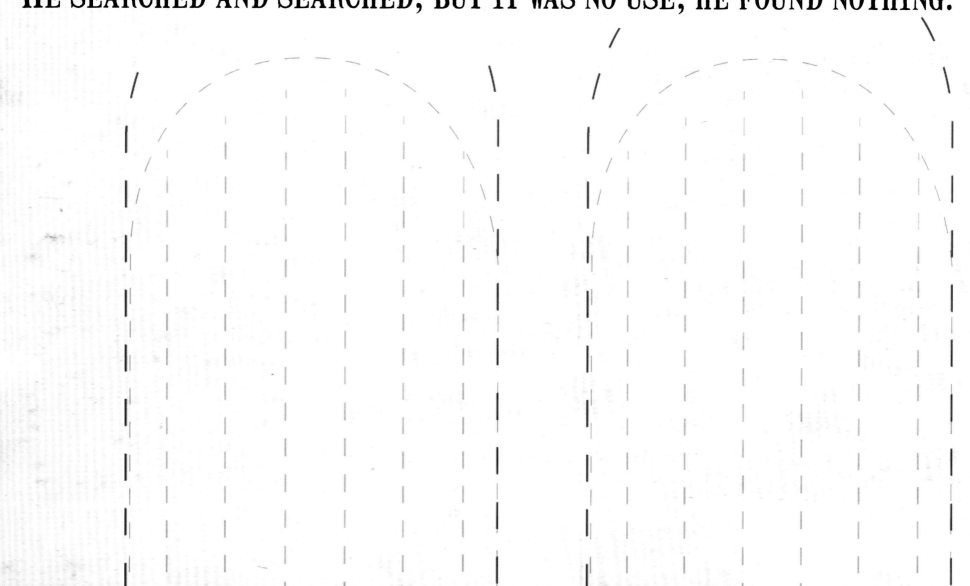

E-NOUGH
AL-READY!

SO DAYS PASSED, HARD TO SAY HOW MANY, BUT MANY MANY DAYS.
THEN ONE MORNING, JUST LIKE THAT,
BRANDISHING HIS ROYAL SWORD, THE KING WENT TEARING DOWNSTAIRS
AND WITH EVERY STEP HE SHOUTED:

I-AM-THE-KING!

KINGS-KNOW-NO-FEAR!

WHAT HE SAW LEFT HIM DUMBSTRUCK
(NOT FOR LONG, JUST FOR A BIT).
IN THE DUNGEON WHERE HE HAD CAST
SOMETHING THERE WAS *SOMETHING ELSE*,

A MUCH BIGGER THING.

GUARDS! TO-THE-AT-TACK!

HE HAD TO DEFEND HIMSELF AGAINST THE MENACING THING. HE STRUGGLED WITH IT, HE TWISTED IT ROUND AND ROUND, HE YANKED IT BACK AND FORTH, AND SUDDENLY THE THING SCATTERED A MILLION *SOMETHINGS* ALL OVER THE PLACE.

THE KING RAN BACK UP THE STAIRS AS FAST AS HE COULD.

RE-TREAT! RE-TREAT! HE SCREAMED.

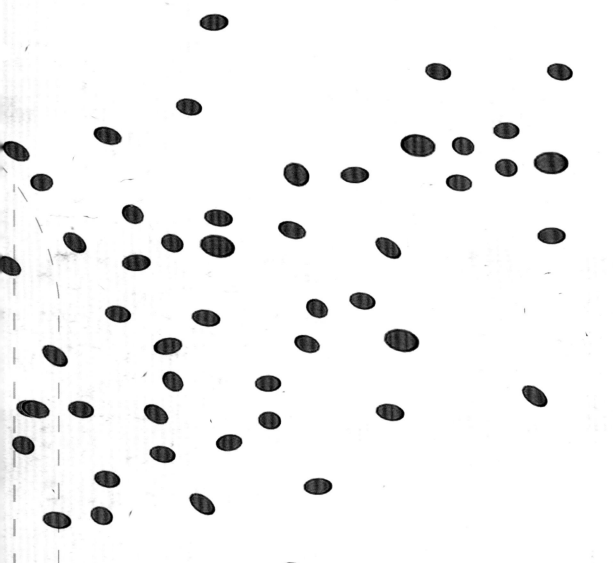

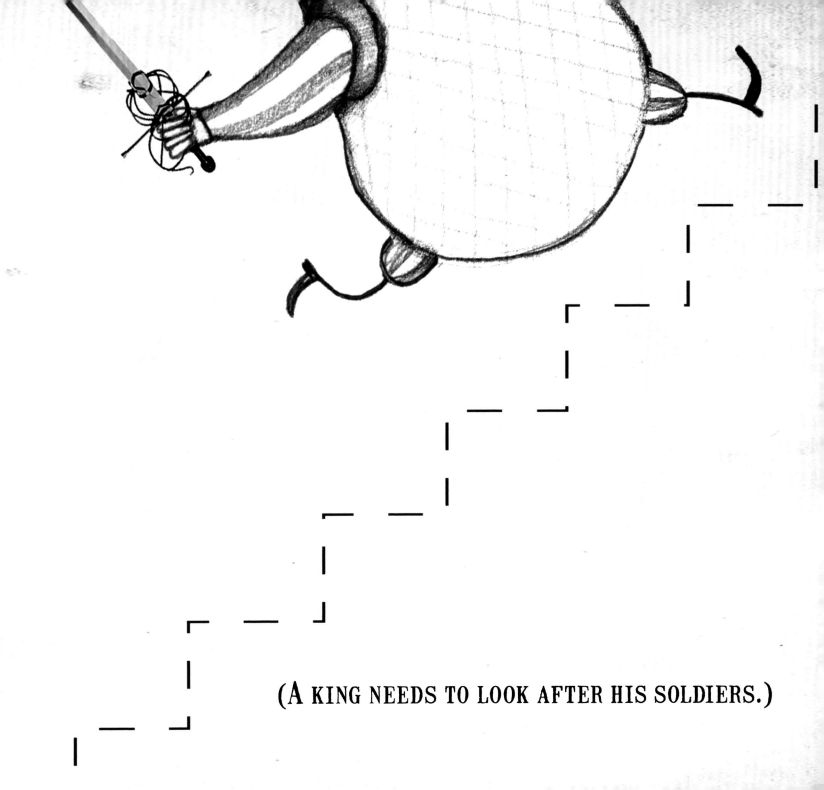

(A KING NEEDS TO LOOK AFTER HIS SOLDIERS.)

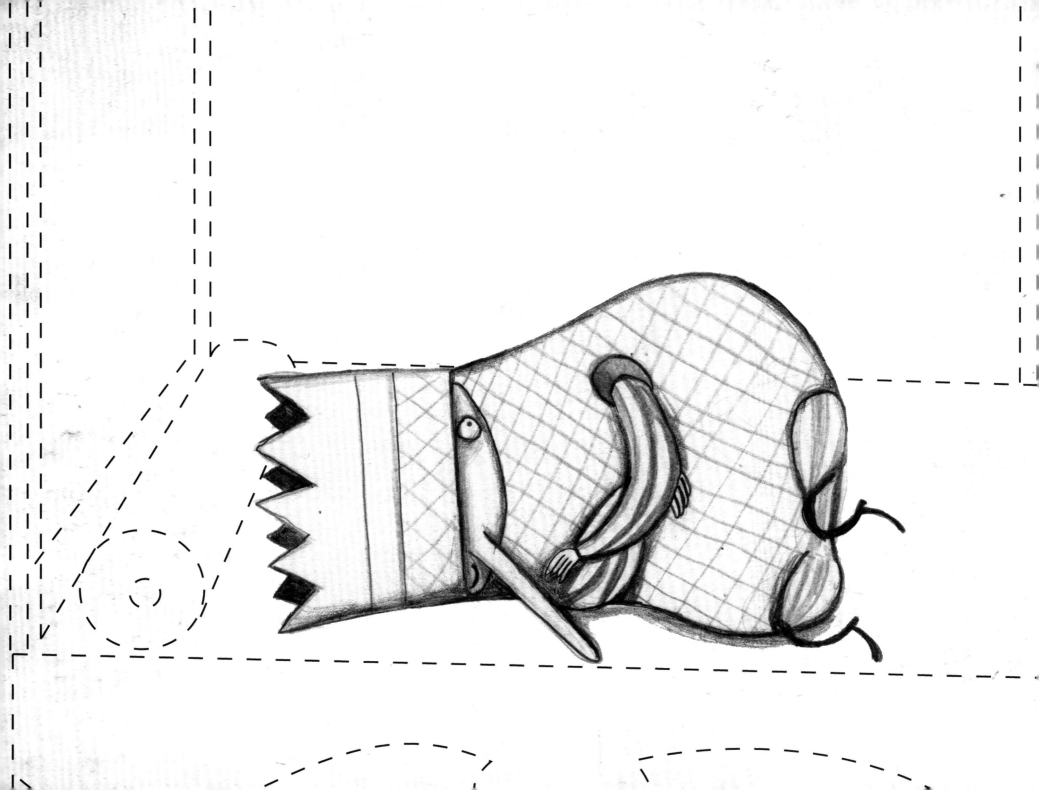

AND ONCE AGAIN, SAFE IN HIS ROOM, HE MUTTERED,
I-AM-THE-KING! I-AM-THE-KING! I-AM! I-AM...!

AND SO AGAIN HE SLEPT.

WHEN HE WOKE UP, AN UNKNOWN

AND UNSETTLING FRAGRANCE WAS FILLING THE WHOLE ROOM, THE WHOLE PALACE, THE WHOLE KINGDOM!

AND THERE BEFORE THE KING'S VERY EYES THOUSANDS AND THOUSANDS OF *THINGS* WERE TURNING OUT LITTLE *SOMETHINGS* THAT WERE TURNING HIS KINGDOM OF NOTHING INTO A KINGDOM OF EVERYTHING.

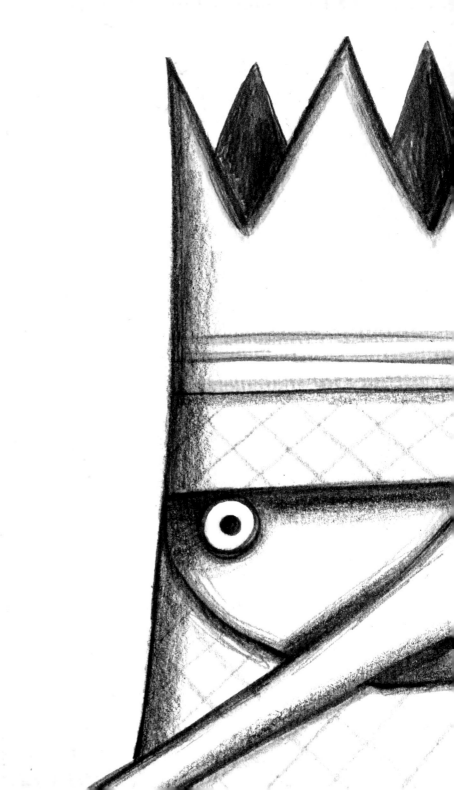

So what did the king do? Nothing.
There wasn't much he could do
except sit and watch
and grin.
Nothing more.
Nothing less.

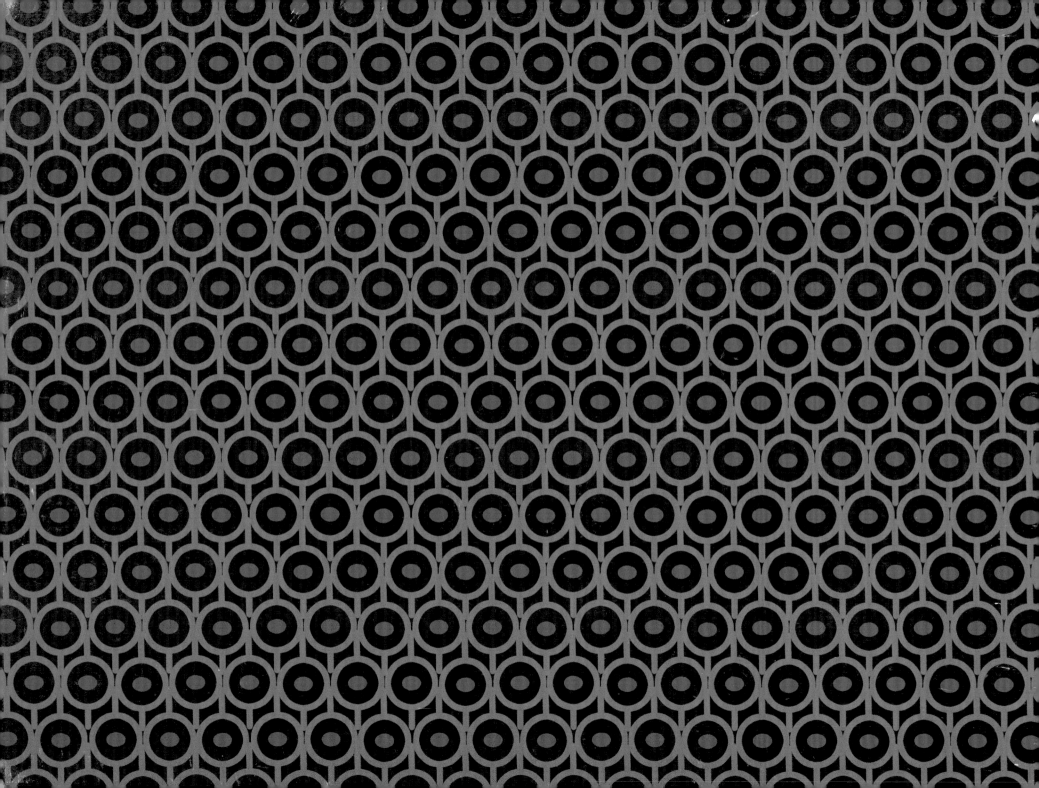